Date: 6/06/2011

BR HILLERT
Hillert, Margaret.
I like things /

I Like Things

by Margaret Hillert
Illustrated by Lois Axeman

DEAR CAREGIVER, The *Beginning-to-Read* series is a carefully written collection of classic readers you may remember from your own childhood. Each book features text comprised of common sight words to provide your child ample practice reading the words that appear most frequently in written text. The many additional details in the pictures enhance the story and offer the opportunity for you to help your child expand oral language and develop comprehension.

Begin by reading the story to your child, followed by letting him or her read familiar words and soon your child will be able to read the story independently. At each step of the way, be sure to praise your reader's efforts to build his or her confidence as an independent reader. Discuss the pictures and encourage your child to make connections between the story and his or her own life. At the end of the story, you will find reading activities and a word list that will help your child practice and strengthen beginning reading skills.

Above all, the most important part of the reading experience is to have fun and enjoy it!

Shannon Cannon

Shannon Cannon,
Literacy Consultant

Norwood House Press • P.O. Box 316598 • Chicago, Illinois 60631
For more information about Norwood House Press please visit our website at
www.norwoodhousepress.com or call 866-565-2900.

LIBRARY OF CONGRESS CATALOGING-IN-PUBLICATION DATA
  Hillert, Margaret.
   I like things / Margaret Hillert ; illustrated by Lois Axeman. — Rev. and
  expanded library ed.
     p. cm. — (Beginning-to-read series)
  Summary: "Easy-to-read text describes collections of familiar items which have
  been arranged by color, size, and shape"—provided by publisher.
   ISBN-13: 978-1-59953-150-2 (library edition : alk. paper)
   ISBN-10: 1-59953-150-X (library edition : alk. paper) [1. Collectors and
  collecting—Fiction. 2. Color—Fiction. 3. Size—Fiction. 4.
  Shape—Fiction.] I. Axeman, Lois, ill. II. Title.
  PZ7.H558Iak 2008
  [E]—dc22
                                          2007034738

I like things.
Big things.
Little things.
Red and yellow
and blue things.

Look here.
Look here.
Here is something I like.
Something pretty.

Look what I can do.
Red, blue, yellow.
I can do it this way.
This is fun.

I can do it this way, too.
Big ones.
Little ones.

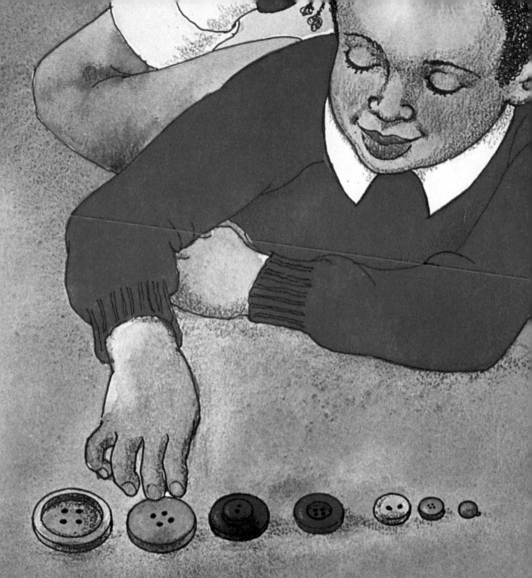

I can do it like this.
Oh, look at this.
This is a good way.

I can make something.
Something for Mother.
It is pretty.
Mother will like it.

Now here is something.
I like this, too.
Father helps me with this.

Oh, look.
Here are good ones.
Good ones for my book.

It is fun to do this,
but I have to work at it.
I find out things, too.
I like to do it.

Here is a good spot to
look for things.
I look and look.
What is here for me?
Guess, guess.

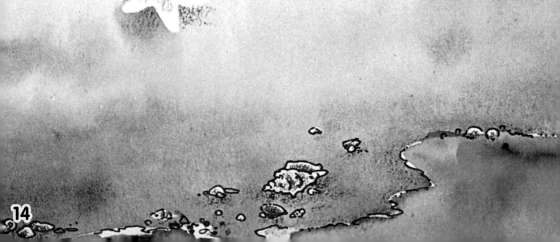

Now, look.
How pretty!
One can go here,
two here, and three here.

And I can do it
this way, too.
It is fun to play like this.

And here is something good.
I have things like this at
my house.

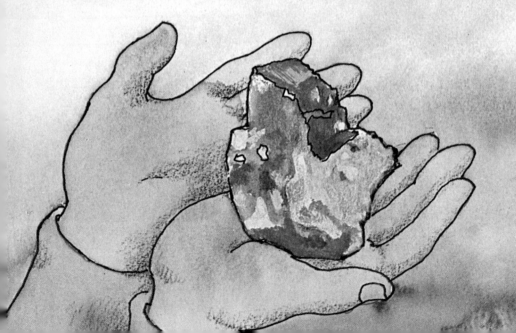

See this
and this
and this.

Look at the one in here.
See how this makes it look.
It looks big, and it looks pretty.

My friend comes to my house
to see what I have.
This is fun.

He wants something that I have.
And look at this.
I want this.

Things are good to have.
But we want something to eat, too.
Father will make something for us.

We will go out to play now.
We will look for things.
We will find things.
What fun we will have!

I like things.
Big things.
Little things.

Red and yellow and
blue things.
What things do *you* like?

READING REINFORCEMENT

The following activities support the findings of the National Reading Panel that determined the most effective components for reading instruction are: Phonemic Awareness, Phonics, Vocabulary, Fluency, and Text Comprehension.

Phonemic Awareness: The /th/ and /t͟h/ sounds

1. Say the word *thumb* and ask your child to repeat the /**th**/ sound.

2. Say the word *that* and ask your child to repeat the /t͟h/ sound.

3. Explain to your child that you are going to say some words and you would like her/him to show you 1 finger if the th sounds like /**th**/ (as in *thumb*) or 2 fingers if the **th** sounds like /t͟h/ (as in *that*).

thing	this	think	bath	three	path
they	them	moth	thread	thin	smooth
the	than	thorn	thirst	math	together

Phonics: /th/ and /t͟h/

1. Demonstrate how to form the letters **t** and **h** for your child.

2. Have your child practice writing **t** and **h** at least three times each.

3. Divide a piece of paper in half by folding it the long way. Draw a line on the fold. Turn it so that the paper has two columns. Write the words *thumb* and *that* at the top of each column.

4. Write the **th** words above on separate index cards. Ask your child to sort the words based on the **th** sounds that correspond to *thumb* and *that*.

Vocabulary: Nouns

1. Explain to your child that nouns are words for people, places and things.

2. Ask your child to page through the book to point out and name the people.

3. Repeat this by asking your child to do the same but pointing out and naming the things in the story.

4. Name the following nouns and ask your child to show 1 finger if it is a person; 2 fingers if it is a thing: buttons, sand, boy, jar, woman, friend, rocks, stamps, man, shells, girl.

5. Ask your child to name other familiar people and things while you show 1 or 2 fingers.

Fluency: Echo Reading

1. Reread the story to your child at least two more times while your child tracks the print by running a finger under the words as they are read. Ask your child to read the words he or she knows with you.

2. Reread the story, stopping after each sentence or page to allow your child to read (echo) what you have read. Repeat echo reading and let your child take the lead.

Text Comprehension: Discussion Time

1. Ask your child to retell the sequence of events in the story.

2. To check comprehension, ask your child the following questions:

   • What are some of the things that the kids in the story like to collect?

   • Which of the collections do you like best? Why? Which would you think would be more fun to collect? Why?

   • How does the girl take care of the things she collects?

   • Do you collect anything? If so, what? If not, what would you like to collect?

I like Things **uses the 64 words listed below.** This list can be used to practice reading the words that appear in the text. You may wish to write the words on index cards and use them to help your child build automatic word recognition. Regular practice with these words will enhance your child's fluency in reading connected text.

a	Father	I	play	us
and	find	in	pretty	
are	for	is		want(s)
at	friend	it	red	way
	fun			we
big		like	see	what
blue	go	little	something	will
book	good	look(s)	spot	with
but	guess			work
		make(s)	that	
can	have	me	the	yellow
comes	he	Mother	things	
	helps	my	this	
do	here		three	
	house	now	to	
eat	how		too	
		oh	two	
		one(s)		
		out		

ABOUT THE AUTHOR Margaret Hillert has written over 80 books for children who are just learning to read. Her books have been translated into many different languages and over a million children throughout the world have read her books. She first started writing poetry as a child and has continued to write for children and adults throughout her life. A first grade teacher for 34 years, Margaret is now retired from teaching and lives in Michigan where she likes to write, take walks in the morning, and care for her three cats.

Photograph by Glenna Washburn

ABOUT THE ADVISER Shannon Cannon contributed the activities pages that appear in this book. Shannon serves as a literacy consultant and provides staff development to help improve reading instruction. She is a frequent presenter at educational conferences and workshops. Prior to this she worked as an elementary school teacher and as president of a curriculum publishing company.